MONSTER MAX
THIS TIME IT'S SIRIUS

ROBIN BENNETT

ILLUSTRATED BY
TOM TINN-DISBURY

Firefly

First published in 2023
by Firefly Press
25 Gabalfa Road, Llandaff North, Cardiff, CF14 2JJ
www.fireflypress.co.uk

Text copyright © Robin Bennett 2023
Illustrations copyright © Tom Tinn-Disbury 2023

A CIP catalogue record of this book is available from the
British Library.

ISBN 978-1-915444-27-1
ebook ISBN 978-1-915444-28-8

This book has been published with the support of the Books
Council of Wales.

Design by Becka Moor

Printed and bound by: CPI Group (UK) Ltd, Croydon,
CR0 4YY

FSC
www.fsc.org
MIX
Paper | Supporting
responsible forestry
FSC® C171272

MONSTER MAX

MAX

THIS TIME IT'S SIRIUS

Robin Bennett: When Robin grew up, he thought he wanted to be a soldier until everyone else realised that putting him in charge of a tank was a very bad idea. He then became an assistant gravedigger, a guy that smashes up houses, private tutor to the rich and famous, entrepreneur ... until finally settling down to write improbable stories to keep his children happy. He once heard himself described on the radio travel news as 'some twit' when his car broke down and blocked the traffic in London. This is about right. Robin is married with three children. He spends his time between France and England.

@writer_robin

Tom Tinn-Disbury: Tom loves to draw (except bicycles, bicycles are really hard to draw!) He lives in Rugby, Warwickshire with his wife, two sons, grumpy dog Wilma and mad cats Sparky & Loki.

tomtinndisbury.com

Dedication

For anything cute and furry
RB

For Harry, another Monster Max in
the making!
T T-D

ALL ABOUT MAX

Max is a very special boy: he can turn himself into a scary, hairy monster by BURPING. And he can turn himself back again by SNEEZING.

This is because he comes from a land

called Krit. Perched on the top of a very pointy mountain, it's the smallest, most hidden country in the world. Also, in Krit, being able to change into a monster, wolf, bear or bat isn't considered unusual at all. Max's mum comes from Krit and she can turn into a wolf.

Sometimes, Max burps by mistake, which can be a nasty surprise if you are standing next to him in the supermarket. And flowers make Max sneeze, so he often finds himself far from home in just his pants.

These days, he's trying to be a better monster … with mixed results.

He's even got a logo:

PROLOGUE

High up in the mountains, the tiny country of Krit was even more hidden than usual.

For it was a dark and stormy night.

Fanghorn, leader of the Red Eye wolves, and fearsome enemy of Monster Max, prowled the chilly corridors of his grim castle, getting crosser by the minute. Fanghorn was a wolf who didn't like people leaving Krit, and that meant Max's mum (and Max). And he also didn't like people who made him look stupid and that also meant Max's mum (and Max).

'They think they're free, running about doing good in this England place!' he snarled. 'But no-one leaves Krit without my permission. I want them here … I want to punish them!'

But how to capture them, when all his efforts had failed so far?

I must have werewolves for this job, he thought. Not just any old ones; I need the strongest and the most loyal.

He burst out onto the castle battlements just as the moon appeared from behind a black cloud, raised his huge jaws into the night, and he howled into the frozen air, 'Bring me the leader of the Varkas pack! Wooooo!'

Almost immediately, he heard answer-ing howls from the ice regions of Krit and it didn't take long for the sound of running feet to reach his wolfish ears.

Fanghorn leapt from the battlements to greet his guest in the castle courtyard.

'Raise the gate!' he snarled at his guards.

But before they got their paws on the lifting lever, there was a terrible splintering noise and the gate exploded into pieces. A wolf raced into the courtyard and came to a screeching stop a whisker away from Fanghorn's nose.

The Varkas pack leader was even bigger than Fanghorn – like the werewolf equivalent of a cage fighter but with extra bits, like teeth and claws. Fanghorn had to stop himself from gulping.

'Yes, sir!' the Varkas wolf barked. (He probably would have saluted if he'd had hands, not four paws.) 'At your service!'

'YES!' said Fanghorn, thinking: these guys are great, they'll always follow orders. 'I have a job for you and for twenty of your best fighters.'

'Sir!'

'You must go to England, to a place called Oxford, and find a Grey Eyed wolf who escaped from Krit, who now calls herself Sally Forbes, and her son, Max. Bring them to me!' Fanghorn turned to go.

'Sir?'

'Yes? What is it?' He turned back to the Varkas wolf impatiently.

'Well, um...' The huge wolf looked embarrassed. 'Did you want us to go, like, right away?'

'Of course, like right away. Otherwise, I would have waited until morning instead of doing this dramatic midnight howling... Anyway, why?'

'It's just that we have a new cub, lovely little fella, and my wife and I kind of run the pack together – like a family thing, you know – and, what I mean to say, your Royal Highness, is that it gives us a bit of a childcare issue ... um...' He stopped as Fanghorn glared at him in furious silence.

'Well, take the cub along – everyone

travels with kids these days. You'll probably get a discount.'

'Sir!' The Varkas pack leader looked relieved. 'Thank you, sir! So, twenty vicious wolves wot know no mercy and are extremely terrifying, against one kid and his mum?'

'Yes... Anything wrong with that?'

'Er, no, sir.' The huge wolf looked a bit unsure but wasn't going to push his luck with Fanghorn's terrible temper. 'Consider thems got!'

The Varkas wolf turned and leapt.

'Wait, hold on ... argh! RAISE THE GATE!' Fanghorn barked at the guards, who had only just finished sticking the broken pieces together with rope and glue. He was too late. There was an awful crashing noise like a small meteorite ploughing through a forest as the Varkas leader smashed the gate all over again.

'Oh, for heaven's sake. Don't these Varkas ever use doors like normal werewolves?' Fanghorn growled. He watched the warrior disappear into the night and, instead of dwelling on his broken gate, he thought about what he would do when he finally had his captives in Krit.

Fanghorn slowly grinned with several dozen very large fangs. He couldn't wait to get his teeth into them.

1

TROUBLE COMES IN TREES

Back in the relative normality of England, two boys made their way through quiet streets. They were on a mission.

'It was a dark and stormy night, da, da, daaaaaaa!' said Max.

Max's joint best friend, Peregrine, looked at Max down his long nose and frowned at him.

'No, it's not. The moon's so bright it's practically daylight – you can even see Sirius, which is actually the brightest star in the night sky. It's sometimes called the Dog Star...'

'OK, Mr Dull of Blimey You're so Boring Land. I'm just trying to make things more interesting,' said Max, looking around for his other joint best friend, his cat Frankenstein, who he suspected was having a better time eating smelly leftovers and terrifying local dogs than he was right now, having to listen to Peregrine going on about stars.

'Well, you should be concentrating on tonight's mission. It's very important,' muttered Peregrine.

'What, helping you build a treehouse in the dark? It just sounds like something that would be easier in the day.'

'Look, if I'm going to finish our new Secret Lair Treehouse, I'm going to need to do it under the cover of darkness. For some reason adults don't like eleven-year-olds carrying about military-grade surveillance units and high-tension electronic cabling in broad daylight… It makes them ask difficult-to-answer questions. And I need you to help carry all this stuff.'

'Still a bit boring.'

'But necessary. I've been up here a lot over the last few weeks and the woods don't seem quite … right.'

'What do you mean?'

'I don't know, maybe it's nothing but I haven't seen any rabbits for ages – there's usually loads hopping about – and there were some claw marks on a tree near here.'

'It wasn't me.'

'I know. Yours are bigger and these didn't seem random. It was almost as if the marks meant something – like they were a message.'

'Creepy.'

'A bit suspicious – so that's why we need to finish the Treehouse Lair. Fanghorn's not going to leave you alone forever. He's been plotting for sure. We need a base of our own – one that's not your parents' kitchen.'

'OK, this Secret Lair Treehouse does sound necessary,' Max admitted. 'But you can see my point. It's hardly Protecting and Doing Good Stuff – more like Creeping about Doing Nerdy Stuff – your speciality…'

He paused as Frankenstein appeared

on a wall in silhouette with something probably very old and definitely very disgusting sticking out of his mouth.

'Anyway...' Max continued, 'it's still long past our bedtimes and those trees over there look pretty sinister. Anything could be lurking in them ... watching us ... just waiting until our backs are turned...'

'No, you can't turn into a monster.'

'Oh.'

'And you've really got to get over this fear of the dark thing.'

'Why? It's like asking an astronaut to get over this lack of oxygen thing. The dark's really scary. Fact.'

'You're a five-hundred-kilo monster – about a third of the time,' said Peregrine. 'You shouldn't be scared of anything.'

'And you're bossier than my teacher – all of the time,' muttered Max.

'We're here,' said Peregrine, ignoring him. They'd come to the end of a track in the woods. A tall antenna, next to what looked like a water tower on metal legs, swayed in the breeze. Peregrine pulled off his rucksack and fished about inside for his tools. 'I've got to get the cameras and radar set up around the treehouse. I'm going to use that old TV antenna to bounce the signal off – perfect. Remember, we're undercover: so no chit-chat and absolutely no monstering unless I need you to lift or bend something heavy. And if anyone comes along, tell them we're walking Frankenstein.'

'Suppose,' muttered Max. He looked about. They had trudged fairly deep into the woods above Oxford and were standing in a clearing with four large oaks at each corner. 'Can I climb up into the treehouse, at least?'

'N-uh-uh … nope.' Peregrine was busy fiddling with some wires, a torch in his mouth. 'S'not really ready, you'll probably fiddle with things… You keep a lookout down here. Let me know if anyone is coming.'

Max sighed. This was going to be a long, dull night.

But, to his surprise, after a bit, Max began to enjoy himself. Even when he wasn't being huge and hairy, with great big teeth like a sabre-toothed tiger, he still had all his monster super-senses. He could smell far-off chimney smoke that made him think of fireworks and Halloween just around the corner; he could see beyond the woods, through gently moving trees, all the way to the River Thames, winding its way like a silver road; and he could hear … whimpering?

'Pssst!' pssted Max, but Peregrine seemed totally fascinated by a pile of old circuit boards. 'Pssst, pssst, ahem. Oi!'

'What?' His friend finally looked up, glaring at Max.

'Did you hear that?'

'I can't hear anything with you shouting your head off every five minutes.'

Max pointed theatrically towards a really dark patch of trees. 'There's something in the bushes.'

'Well, go and take a look.' Peregrine went back to what he'd been doing.

Max sighed. The trees were dark, but he wouldn't burp, he told himself. Peregrine was right – he should save turning into a monster for special occasions. Just then, Frankenstein came slinking over.

'Come on,' said Max, to his cat. 'But you go first.'

Frankenstein seemed to shrug as if to say fine, whatever, and began to creep cattily in the direction of the gentle whimpering.

Max followed. They crept towards the old water tower, looming in the darkness like an alien on stilts. Max's sharp eyes could make out something small and round nestling in the leaves by one of the metal feet.

As he got closer, the crying noises stopped, almost as if whatever was making them had heard Max and was holding its breath, waiting…

Max forgot his fear and crept past Frankenstein, who had gone very still, his skinny back arched, his hair beginning to stand on end.

'It's OK,' Max whispered, although whether he was talking to Frankenstein or to whatever was hiding in the grass he wasn't sure.

Max took one step forward, then another and another. He looked down at what he had found and scratched his head.

'Peregrine,' he said, and this time there was something in his voice that made his friend look up right away. 'I think you should come over here and look at this.'

Two bright eyes set in a fluffy face looked up at Max, Peregrine and Frankenstein, and blinked. The puppy had stopped crying but Max could see it was trembling.

He leant down, extending his hand slowly and stroked its fur. That did the trick – the puppy stopped shaking and licked Max's hand instead.

'It likes me,' said Max. 'Let's keep him.'

'Hmmm,' Peregrine didn't sound so sure. 'It must be lost, but someone will be looking for it.'

'We can teach it tricks, but first it needs a name,' Max declared, ignoring Peregrine. Something made him look up at the sky. 'What was the name of that star again, the really bright one, up there?'

'Sirius,' answered Peregrine.

'That's a good name for him, as you said it's the Dog Star.'

'Except this isn't a dog,' said Peregrine.

'Of course it is,' Max said. 'It's got four legs and a tail. It's fluffy and licky.'

'Yes, but look at those ears, the shape of its head and the size of its paws.'

'What about them? You're not going

to convince me it's a guinea pig.'

'No,' said Peregrine, peering closer. 'It's a wolf.'

Both friends looked at the wolf cub and thought their own private thoughts.

Frankenstein hissed, making Sirius growl back in a cute puppy way and show his tiny pointed teeth.

'Aw, they hate each other... Sweet,' said Max. 'I still think we should keep him.'

'I really don't think that's a good idea. It's been proved through scientific study that wolves cannot be tamed, even if they spend time with humans.' Peregrine pushed his glasses further up his nose, something he always did when preparing to make a speech. 'The real question here, of course, is what a wolf is doing on its own in the middle of Oxfordshire, not whether it would make a good pet. It's far from its natural habitat, the nearest being central Europe...'

'Shh,' said Max.

'No, you shush, I was talking.'

'I can hear something running ...

actually lots of somethings running …
and very fast … towards us.'

'Max…'

BURP!

'Gres?'

'Well, I was going to say, now would
be a good time to turn into a monster,
but – for once – you're ahead of me.'

'Grankyu.'

'Don't mention it, now can we go?'

'Grot about Gririus?'

'Sirius stays,' said Peregrine firmly.

'Might be grery grangerous for the
grittle furball.'

'Sorry, no time to argue, it's time
to show you my Bionic Utility Tall
Trousers.'

'You mean your BUTT, hee hee?'

'See you back at HQ!' shouted

Peregrine, pressing a button on his belt. His trousers suddenly shot him into the air until he was twice the height of Monster Max.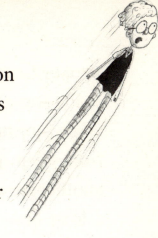

'Be careful!' cried Max.

With that, Peregrine stepped over several small trees as if they weren't there and raced off into the night.

Max looked around and listened hard. The sound of running feet had slowed but his monster senses told him danger was close. Very close. Frankenstein was nowhere to be seen, which was a relief, and Sirius was looking at him expectantly, not seeming in the least worried that Max had just turned from a small boy into a large monster. Just in case he was about to get scared, Max stroked Sirius, who nibbled Max's claws as if it was a game.

His monster ears picked up a growl from deep in the woods. Followed by another growl: low and very scary. Then a long drawn-out howl that sounded like anger mixed with pain.

Monster Max stepped in front of Sirius protectively, searched the clearing and saw a large bit of fallen tree, which he picked up. He also saw a rusty metal gate, which he picked up in his other paw, just in case.

'Gright,' he said, scowling into the trees, Peregrine might have told him to escape, but he was Monster Max. 'To Grotect and do Good Stuff!' he roared into the night, just as something very fast and very strong shot out of the darkness and hit him harder than he'd ever been hit in his whole monstering life.

'Roar!' roared Max and threw the gate. There was a loud metal DOINK noise and something yelped in pain.

Max was just about to run after the shape, when something else, almost as big as Max and almost as hairy, hit him from behind, even harder than before. It was like being run into by a shaggy lorry.

Max swung his tree at the running shape … and missed.

Instead, he hit the water tower, which swayed one way … swayed another … creaked … then toppled…

Right on top of Max.

His world went black.

2

THE VARKAS PACK

When Max woke, he was in his bed at home, back to being ordinary Max, aged eleven, who liked cowboy movies and lived with his parents, Sally and Peter Forbes. The sun was shining and birds twittered politely in the friendly trees that lined their street.

Max had a bit of a headache but checked all his arms and legs and decided he was, on the whole, OK considering he'd had several tons of metal land on his head a few hours ago. Luckily, monsters have skulls like concrete bunkers.

He remembered blacking out, then waking up just before dawn still under a mountain of junk. Whoever his attackers were, they must have run off, thanks to all the falling metal. Sensing that the danger had passed, Max had brushed off a couple of girders and the main bit of the old water tank, then clambered out of the pile.

The dusty ground made him sneeze, which turned him back to being Max the boy – and a rather cold boy, at that. He had tottered home a bit unsteadily in his torn shirt and the trousers he found on the ground. He would go back later, when it got dark, and tidy up.

Right now he needed breakfast and answers. In that order.

'Morning!'

Max was used to finding Peregrine at their breakfast table when he came downstairs. His friend practically lived there during the holidays.

Peregrine was tucking into a large bowl of milky porridge but Max could smell bacon…

'Ah, Max!' His father turned from the cooker, wearing an apron with clouds on it. His father liked clouds in the way frogs love hopping. 'Peregrine was telling me about last night – bit of a worry if there's wolves about. I was going to wait until your mother came back and we could put our heads together and decide what to do. In the meantime, you look like you need a cooked breakfast.'

'Yes, please, Dad!' said Max, eyeing the orange juice. 'Where is she?'

'Well, your mother and Madame Pinky-Ponky have taken up balloon ballet. Your mother thinks Madame Pinky-Ponky spends too much time in the house.'

'It sounds dangerous.' Max was worried – Madame Pinky-Ponky was the closest thing he had to a granny. She was also a genius at making cakes, but that was beside the point. 'She's probably about a hundred and ten years old. Shouldn't she be doing something with, you know, more sitting down … and wool?'

'Sitting down is where things start to go wrong in my view!' His mum came in looking flushed, followed by Madame Pinky-Ponky, who was grinning from one wrinkly ear to the other. 'Anyway, we had a fantastic time. Madame Pinky-Ponky got top marks for her high altitude brisé.'

'I 'ad a lovely time,' said Madame P. 'Thank you, dear. Now I think I need a long bath and a lie down, if you'll excuse me.'

'What's that I heard about wolves as we were coming up the stairs?' Max's mum was swilling around the remains of the coffee in the pot, looking like she was deciding if there was enough for one more cup or if she needed to make more. But Max could tell she was watching him out of the corner of her eye. Anything about wolves was bound to fascinate her – it was a pretty badly-kept family secret that she could turn into a beautiful grey wolf as easily as Max could turn himself into a not very beautiful monster.

'Well,' said Max, deciding not to mention anything about the encounter with something very fast and very strong until he knew more, 'I'm still not convinced it was a wolf. It might have been a puppy.'

'OK, what about the pointy ears, the running feet, the growls and that scary howl I heard when I left…?' mentioned Peregrine.

'Using your magic BUTT?'

'Precisely. So how do you explain that howl?'

'Er, I, um… OK, so Mum, Dad, I guess, if you put it like that, we might have a bit of a wolf problem.'

'Just as we thought,' said his dad.

'What colour was the cub's fur?' asked his mum, sitting down.

'Almost all black, except he has a sort of grey "V" on his back,' said Max, making Peregrine look sharply at him. His friend opened his mouth to ask something awkward, but was stopped by a crash.

Max's mum had just dropped her mug.

Spilt coffee ran across the table and dripped on the floor. Max's parents looked at each other in silence for a few seconds.

'You're sure about the grey V-shaped

fur, Max?' she asked quietly.

'Yes.' Max was very sure.

'Varkas pack,' his worried-looking parents both said at the same time.

And whatever that was, it didn't sound good.

Five minutes later, they were in their library.

Max's dad swept aside the plans and drawings for Peregrine's Secret Lair Treehouse, making space on the table for Max's favourite book, Kritters of Krit.

He turned to 'W' (for Witches, Werewolves and Wobble Monsters). Max might have been interested to know more about Wobble Monsters but his parents and Peregrine had other ideas. His dad's finger traced down the different werewolf clans until it got to 'V'. There was a single entry. Max read it over his mum's shoulder.

'Varkas Pack'

Strongest of all the Red Eye wolves, they inhabit the highest, coldest places in Krit, where only Ice Witches and Rock Giants can normally survive. The Varkas pack have long been considered the elite soldiers of the Red Eye wolf clan: fast, fearsome and brave. It is said that if one is your enemy, you should be very afraid … but they are also known for being great defenders of their friends and loyal to anyone who truly wants the best for Krit.

Below there was a picture of an adult and also a cub. The cub looked exactly like Sirius.

Footnote:
Varkas cubs, like all werewolves of Krit, are not able to take their human form until they reach the age of thirteen.

Peregrine was the first to speak. 'That's them,' he said shortly.

'You're sure?' asked Mrs Forbes.

Peregrine nodded. 'Uh huh.'

Max's parents frowned at this.

'Fanghorn is up to something,' said his dad.

'If he's sending Varkas wolves, he's getting really angry. Max, you'll have to be careful – even when you're a monster, this wolf pack will be really dangerous. I think it's likely they will be looking to capture you and take you to Krit and they might hurt you getting there.'

'Don't worry,' said Max. 'I'll be careful.' He was thinking about the night before and how what he thought was a wolf had knocked him off his feet but, if he said anything, he'd be grounded for sure.

It was all very well having an enemy who lived at the top of a secret mountain (Krit) several hundred miles away and not really that scary (especially if you can turn into a monster) but if they started sending really strong wolves over to get you and (worst of all) your family, then that was another thing…

'At least they don't know where we live.' Max's dad cut across Max's gloomy thoughts. 'Which means we're safe here.'

'Agreed,' said Max's mum. 'They'll also do their best to stay out of town. They're wild animals when they're in wolf form, not comfortable around busy places. But if they lose their fear or something forces them to come into town, they'll find us eventually and we'll have a real problem.' She turned to the boys. 'OK, I hate to say this, but you two need to lie low for a bit. They don't know England and Oxford. If they can't find us here, they'll move on. Varkas never stay in one place for long. So we keep our heads down and we should be fine.'

'OK, Mrs Forbes,' said Peregrine. 'I can get on with the Secret Lair Treehouse.'

'OK, Mum,' said Max, a little too quietly.

After breakfast had been cleared away and Peregrine had gone home, Max grabbed the last two bits of bacon out of the pan and went up to his room via the secret staircase. He didn't want to bump into anyone.

Once in his room he looked about.

It was just the same as he had left it. The morning sun still poured through the window, his bed looked messy and he could hear children playing football in the park across the street. He fished about in his pocket and went over to the cupboard.

Two black eyes looked out from a comfy nest of woolly jumpers, a fluffy tail wagged and a little pink mouth yawned.

'Good morning, Sirius Sleepy Head,' said Max, feeling happy but guilty all at the same time. 'I hope you like bacon.'

A WEREWOLF'S NOT JUST
FOR HALLOWEEN

Truth was, Max hadn't taken Sirius home on purpose.

When the water tower had fallen on his head, the last thing he remembered doing was putting his big monster body over the small cub to protect him. When he'd woken, hours later, Sirius had been curled up in Max's fur, fast asleep.

It had been cold and Max really

hadn't had the heart to leave him out there with no shelter all on his own.

'I know I can't keep you,' he said now. 'Your parents will be worried. Plus I don't think Frankenstein likes you.' Sirius nibbled Max's fingers, then rolled over to have his little round tummy rubbed. 'We'll go back tonight,' he decided. 'Tidy up the mess and look for your parents. Peregrine won't be there; he's visiting his granny.'

Later, a long time after supper, when the house was quiet, Max snuck down to the kitchen and opened the fridge.

'Ah, ha!' he grinned, helping himself to three thick slices of cold ham, a jar of pickled onions, several cheese slices, four boiled eggs, a pint of milk and some leftover cheesecake from supper the day before.

He grabbed some bread before tiptoeing up the secret staircase and back to his room.

'Midnight monstering is hungry work,' he explained to Sirius, as he shared out their carpet picnic. 'BUUUUURRRRPPPPP!' he burped. 'Gralso grelps you burp.'

Sirius started to run around in excited circles and wag his little tail – not in the least startled that (once again) Max had just turned into a seven-foot monster with teeth like walrus tusks.

'Woo woooo!' Sirius gave a miniature howl.

'Shhhhhoooofff…' said Monster Max putting a clawed finger to his toothy mouth. 'Grokay, grokay, grittle guy, gret's go. Grankenstein, coming?'

Frankenstein, who'd spent the day sleeping on a cushion by Max's window, looked up, looked at Sirius and shook his head.

'Shoot yourshelf,' said Monster Max, not surprised, but a bit disappointed. He'd have to work on making them friends at some stage.

Sirius looked like he enjoyed springing out of Max's special, extra-wide Monstering Skylight that Peregrine had rigged up for him. It opened up at the back of their house, where Monster Max could exit without being watched by nosy neighbours. He also seemed to love peeking out of Max's knapsack as they bounded across the rooftops at such great speed that if anyone did look out of their window, they would have just seen a sort of furry blur.

'Probably a big squirrel,' they would tell themselves, because the human brain, presented with the sight of a giant orange monster skipping over the tops of the houses opposite, basically sticks its fingers in its ears, closes its eyes and goes 'La la la!' until it comes up with something more reasonable ... you know, like squirrels.)

When they got to the edge of the

town, Max jumped off the roof of the last house and took a peak inside the knapsack at Sirius.

The cub lay fast asleep on Max's spare clothes.

Monster Max made sure no one was about, then shot across the fields that separated the town from the woods, startling a couple of pheasants and a fox … but otherwise unnoticed.

'Gree hee,' said Monster Max to himself as he got to the Secret Lair Treehouse and the shattered remains of the water tower. Being a boy on his own in dark woods was one thing, being a monster was quite another and he knew which he preferred. He was Monster Max the Amazing – strong as ten lions, cunning as several foxes, stealthy like a ninja – he was invincible and invisible, he was…

'I thought you said treehouses were nerdy.'

The not-so-undetectable Monster Max gave a not-so-monstery yelp and jumped in the air.

'Oh grello, Greregrine,' he said to his friend, who had come out from behind a tree. 'I had no idea you were … such a quiet walker.'

'What?'

'I thought you were at your granny's.'

'She's not very well.' Peregrine stared hard at Monster Max. 'Come to think of it, you don't look so well either? You look a bit pale for a hairy monster … and sort of shifty.' Peregrine took a step closer and Max took a step back.

'What's in your knapsack?'

'Oh, nothing… '

'It looks sort of bulgy?'

Peregrine went to poke it and Max slapped his hand away.

'Ow!'

'Grorry, I thought I saw a mosquito land on your arm.'

'In October?'

'Well, you know, different types of mosquito, grittle blighters, get everywhere, hide out, grobal warming, or might have been a bee or a flying ant…'

'Why are you gabbling? You sound even more idiotic than usual.'

'Grorry. You know me, the dark, on edge…'

'And anyway, why are you here if you thought I wasn't going to be about?'

'Oh.' Monster Max at least had prepared for that. 'I came to do something about the tower, you know. To Grotect and Tidy Up a bit ... hee hee!' He laughed weekly and hoped Sirius wouldn't wake up.

'Well,' Peregrine was still wrinkling his nose suspiciously, 'now you're here, I might as well give you a tour of the Treehouse. I've finished the carpentry, so it's safe to go up, even for monsters. I'll use the ladder. You just jump up that tree.'

'Grighty ho,' said Max, taking the knapsack with Sirius in it, and placing it under the biggest tree. 'I'll just leave this here. Don't need this silly knapsack.'

'Grolly!' said Monster Max, when he'd got up high above the trees, landing with a bump on the solid wooden platform just as Peregrine arrived via a well-camouflaged ladder.

Max had imagined the Secret Lair Treehouse to be basically a treehouse with a few of Peregrine's latest inventions. In fact, it was more like several trees connected with small walkways between them. Max could make out in the dark that each tree had its own shelter : so it was really more like a Tree Castle.

'Come and have a look in the Command Centre,' said Peregrine. 'Mind your head.'

The Command Centre turned out to be the biggest hut at the top of the tallest tree. Inside it was surprisingly cosy. There was even a rug and two comfy chairs.

'This is the central surveillance hub,' Peregrine pointed at a bank of computer screens, each showing different parts of the forest. 'I've got night-vision cameras dotted everywhere and even a small radar.'

'Gramazing!' said Max, actually very impressed. Peregrine moved away from the screens to a control panel on a desk.

'However, since finding out from

your parents about the Varkas pack, I've been adding defences to the Secret Lair Treehouse, so we've got hidden net bazookas, rope traps, gunk cannons… Are you alright?'

'Grine, grine!' said Monster Max quickly. On one of the screens behind Peregrine, he could see the bag with Sirius in it moving. 'Carry on talking!'

'I personally think these wolves represent the biggest threat so far sent by Fanghorn. I've been reading up in your library. They are cunning, intelligent and very strong – almost as strong as you, Max.'

Monster Max nodded and tried to keep his attention on Peregrine, while still looking at what Sirius was doing via the monitor. The cub had now jumped out of the knapsack, yawned and started peeing against a tree.

'If they are still here,' Peregrine carried on, 'and they find out where you live, they will kidnap your mother and take her back to Fanghorn. They'll probably eat your dad, or whatever Fanghorn has told them to do.'

'What?!' Max was torn between alarm about what the Varkas pack, according to Peregrine, might (or might not) do and what Sirius might (or might not) do.

Right now he had found the ladder and was sniffing the air.

'The Varkas werewolves have got super senses like you, too,' said Peregrine. 'Fantastic night vision and a very good sense of smell.'

That must be true, thought Max, as Sirius could clearly smell where he was. The cub started to climb the ladder in a very wobbly way...

'Neee ah,' said Monster Max.

'What?' said Peregrine.

'Ah, my knee. Ah, ow,' said Monster Max quickly, rubbing his knee. 'Bumped it.' There was a pause. Sirius was almost all the way up the ladder.

'You're in a very strange mood tonight,' said Peregrine. 'And I'm tired after sawing wood all day, so I'll go home now, I think. Leave you to your tidying up.'

Peregrine started to turn just as Sirius'

fluffy face appeared through the open door at the top on the ladder.

'Grood idea! Grotta go to work, grerry interesting treehouse, Grerigrine, grank you!'

Max bounded past Peregrine, leapt into the air, scooping up Sirius before Peregrine could spot him, and launched himself out of the treehouse to the ground.

He just had time to shove Sirius back in the bag, before Peregrine came down the ladder.

'Well, enjoy yourself,' said Peregrine, switching on a complicated pair of night-vision goggles. 'Don't do anything I wouldn't do.'

'Course not,' said Monster Max, trying not to look suspicious. 'Grighty night!'

As Peregrine disappeared into the dark, Max slumped against a tree, his heart beating very fast.

That had been close.

GOODBYE

When Max was sure Peregrine had really gone, he took Sirius out of the knapsack.

Sirius jumped up and tried to lick Monster Max's nose off.

'Grerrof, urgh,' said Monster Max. 'You're a very bad werewolf. You nearly got me into a lot of trouble!'

Sirius wasn't in the least bit concerned. He could tell Max wasn't really cross.

'Gright, we need to get to work,

gren...' Max felt a little lump in his heart appear, like it had just got a bit heavier. 'Gren we'll see if we can't get you back where you belong, I gress.'

With Monster Max's strength and speed, tidying up the twisted metal from the water tower was easy and quick. Sirius kept busy by going around the place sniffing.

There was also a lot of general rubbish lying about the tower and a big pile of concrete. So Monster Max dug a hole, his huge monster claws scooping up mounds of earth. He had to keep stopping though, as Sirius insisted on helping, which basically meant he got buried every few seconds and Max had to fish him out.

When the hole was done, Max put

all the concrete and rubbish in it and covered it up.

This just left him with a pile of metal from the water tower's legs, the water container and some thick metal wires.

'Watch gris!' Monster Max said, and he sucked up the metal cable like spaghetti, then he popped the broken metal container in his mouth. 'Mmm, grummy,' he said, swallowing it with a lot of clanky metal sounds.

'Yap, yap!' Sirius went over to sniff a pile of twisted poles in case they were edible too.

'Not for you,' said Monster Max, picking up Sirius and leaping onto the top of a tree.

He wasn't sure what he was looking for – some sign of Sirius' parents perhaps? Not that he was particularly looking forward to meeting them again. His shoulder was still sore from where one of them had bashed into him.

Sirius wriggled in his arms and tried to lick his face again, then tried to jump down.

'Careful,' said Max and, to keep the werewolf cub amused, he burped again – a huge belch that made the metal bolts from the container he'd just swallowed shoot out of his mouth like machinegun bullets. 'Pretty cool, huh?' said Monster Max.

Sirius seemed to agree, but then he yawned. Max looked at the moon, which had moved right across the sky since they had arrived. They'd been there a long time.

'Sleepy?' He knew that puppies needed a lot of rest.

Sirius blinked. A bit like a 'yes'.

'Grokay,' said Max, jumping down from the tree.

It didn't take long to find the spot in which Sirius had been whimpering when Max had found him.

'Grere you go,' he said, laying the fluffy cub down on the soft leaves. Sirius gave another huge yawn and curled up. 'G'right!' said Monster Max, straightening up, his monster ears straining into the night. For a few minutes, there was nothing out of the ordinary: an owl in a nearby wood, a chip van a few streets away shutting up for the night, a bus changing gear as it went up a hill ... and the faintest sound of paws. Running. Growling noises.

Monster Max's fur started to stand on end, which it always did when there was danger approaching.

The Varkas pack was coming!

He was glad he was still a monster – that way he could make a quick escape before being seen.

He looked down at Sirius sleeping peacefully in the moonlight. Perhaps a bit of dust got into his eye – that was woods for you – or perhaps it was something else. Either way, as Max turned to go, he felt sad he was leaving his new friend, but happy that his folks seemed to be coming for him.

'Goodbye, grittle fella, I'll miss you.' Monster Max turned and walked through a thorn bush without noticing.

As Max mooched away, head down, Sirius woke and watched him go with small, intelligent eyes.

Monster Max got to a handy hedgerow, then took out the Emergency Monster Pack his mum insisted he carry in his fur. It had sneezing powder (for turning back into Max, the boy), a spare set of clothes and a ten-pound note.

One sneeze and, a few minutes later,

the boy Max started to trudge home, feeling sad, but quite sure he'd done the right thing … right up until he got to his front door.

Because Sirius was waiting for him on the step.

'Woo-wooo,' the wolf cub said, in a sort of miniature but very cute howl. Then he tried to jump up but fell off the step.

'How did you—?' Max scooped him up. 'You should be with your pack and your parents.' He held Sirius up to his face and put on his sternest look. 'You're a bad werewolf!'

Sirius nibbled Max's nose.

'No, I'm not falling for that again. I'm taking you back tomorrow. First thing!'

But by the time he had got back into the house, back into his bedroom and settled Sirius for the night in his cupboard, Max had convinced himself it wasn't a good idea to leave him in the woods again.

Perhaps what he heard wasn't them coming for their cub after all … but the wolves leaving? Like Mum said, the Varkas pack never stayed in one place for very long. They always kept on the move.

He would keep an eye out for those wolves, Max decided, and hand Sirius over in person – even if it might be dangerous. But no more leaving the cub on his own. For now, Sirius would have to remain a secret.

Max lay in his bed and thought about things.

There was the secret of the really strong werewolf hurting Max, the secret of the Varkas pack – probably sent by Fanghorn – still being in the woods around Oxford and now the secret of Sirius.

Secrets were piling up like old metal rusting in the woods … and it could all come crashing down at any moment.

It took him ages to fall asleep.

BUTT FIREWORKS

WEEEEEE … BANG!

Frankenstein gave a sort of surprised yeow! and shot through a hole in the wooden panelling of the library – a hole that Max suspected was another way to get to the secret staircase.

Oh, dear, thought Max, just when his cat (and joint best friend) was getting over having Sirius around, firework night had come along.

'Frankenstein hates fireworks,' he explained to a puzzled-looking Sirius, who had padded over to inspect the hole. 'He'll probably stay in the cellar hunting mice and spiders for a day or two, then make out that nothing happened. I think he's a bit embarrassed.'

Madame Pinky-Ponky was 'babysitting' Max while his parents went to a party across town. Max had been invited but he had asked if he could go to the fireworks at the football ground down the road instead.

'Don't eat too many toffee apples,' his father had said. 'You remember what happened last time?' Dad shook his head. 'Not that anyone could forget what happened last time, least of all the people below us on the big wheel – it went in their hair and everything.'

'Dad! It wasn't last time: I was four!'

'Stop picking on Max, darling. It's true, he was very little and those apples were very big. And your mother told me you were sick on holiday in Skegness and it dripped through the grating of an iron walkway and people below were in pedalos…'

'Mum, Dad, can we stop talking about this now. I'm eating.'

'No, you're not.'

'No, but I plan to later: toffee apples and loads of them.'

'Come on, darling, or we'll be late,' said Max's mum to his dad. 'Max, be careful. I've been getting a funny feeling we're being watched. Call it a wolf's instinct.'

'Um,' said Max.

'Sorry,' said Peregrine, when Max

rang him to ask if he wanted to meet at the football ground later. 'No can do. I'm finishing up the Secret Lair Treehouse tonight. Getting the steel doors on is going to make a bit of noise, and I'm counting on the racket from the fireworks to cover it up.'

'OK,' said Max. 'Can't wait to see it.'

'My best work yet,' said Peregrine proudly and put the phone down.

'Right.' Max turned to Sirius. 'Looks like you'll be able to come after all. Are you sure you're not going to be scared of fireworks?'

'Grrrrr,' said Sirius, looking small but very brave.

That's one big difference about having a werewolf for a pet, thought Max as he packed his Emergency

Monster Pack and put on a warm coat: they understand everything you say. I wonder what he'll be like when he can talk and turn into a human? We'll be great friends, probably.

As expected, Sirius was a big hit with all the people Max bumped into at the funfair before the fireworks got going. He got his ears scratched, his tummy tickled and lots of tasty morsels from people's hotdogs and burgers. They went on the dodgems together and the mini big wheel, then won a coconut, because Max was quite good at throwing things, even when he wasn't a colossal monster.

'Here,' said Max as they walked away, 'these grow on palm trees and you can eat them.' Before Max could stop him, Sirius tried to bite the coconut. 'No, wait, you have to break it open first!' Max looked about and saw some giant bins by a group of trees. 'I'll show you!'

As soon as they got behind the biggest bin, Max burped.

'Grockie dokie,' he said, splitting the coconut easily with his claws. 'Try this.' It was great not having Peregrine around to tell him not to turn into a monster.

Sirius loved lapping up the milk from his half of the coconut, but didn't seem to like the nutty white bit, which he spat out.

'Pah, pah, pah!'

'Here,' said Monster Max, handing the thirsty wolf cub his coconut half. 'Grink mine.'

As Sirius lapped away at the sweet milk, Max couldn't resist looking in the bin. Hmmm, grummy, thought Monster Max.

A few moments later Monster Max had eaten: several burger wrappings, soggy sandwiches, orange peel, someone's happy meal (even the pointy toy), sausage rolls, cola cans, a hairy toffee, cold coffee, hot dogs (chewed), apple (stewed), nappies (poo'd), Cornish pasties, ice cream goo and a huge pile of…

Wait a sec! His monster senses were suddenly telling him to turn around – right now! In fact, for the last few minutes, he'd been too busy stuffing his face thinking, 'This is great, Sirius doesn't judge me,' to wonder what his friend was up to. Which was why he probably needed to check.

But he was just a second too late. He watched Sirius, his healthy coconut milk finished, cross to a half-eaten stick of candyfloss, open his jaws as wide as he could and…

'Nooooo!' cried Monster Max, who really didn't think candyfloss would be good for werewolves.

Too late: Sirius took a huge puppy bite out of the super-sweet pink cloud on a stick.

And Max could not have been more right about candyfloss and wolf cubs.

As the sugar hit his werewolf brain,

with its ancient magic that gave werewolves their power, Sirius froze. His eyes went whirley. He started to vibrate so much that he went sort of fuzzy around the edges.

'Gririus?' said Monster Max, worried.

'Wooooooooooooooooooooooooooo!' howled Sirius and shot off like a fluffy rocket.

'Gro no!' said Monster Max, leaping after him. 'Come back!' he cried, but Sirius, with a sugar rush was unstoppable. He streaked across the fairground, howling, knocking things over, straight into the one place Max had been avoiding all evening.

The Haunted House.

'Gro! Really gro!' groaned Monster Max. Haunted Houses terrified him.

Suddenly he wished Peregrine was here.

Perhaps he could wait outside?

But what if Sirius got hurt? He seemed to remember there was an age restriction on these things. Could it be dangerous?

Max took a deep breath and, ignoring the teenager on the door, ran into the scary darkness.

The next few minutes were confusing and terrifying.

For everyone.

The people already inside suddenly found they were sharing a dark, cramped space with a large hairy monster and something howling like a werewolf. People started rushing out screaming, followed by Sirius, who'd

somehow got his jaws into a large sausage, followed by Monster Max who was also screaming because he'd got spider web in his eyes and had stubbed his toe on a metal thing.

'BOOM!' the first firework went off.

Sirius swallowed the sausage whole and raced towards the fenced-off area where they were set out.

The first thing Max's amazing monster eyes saw once he'd got the remainder of the web out of his eyes was a large rocket streaking across the sky and – attached to it – a small werewolf.

'Gaaahhhh!' he cried in horror and jumped.

Luckily the sky was dark and the people on the ground didn't have Max's incredible night vision, or they would have been stunned (and probably pretty impressed) by the sight of a huge orange monster catching a small puppy in mid-air with one hand, and popping a rocket in its mouth with the other, which exploded with a sort of muffled bang.

Purple and red sparks shot out of Monster Max's bottom as they sailed off into the night sky and landed with a soft flump in some trees far away from the fair and fireworks.

On the way home a very tired (and happy) Sirius fell asleep in Max's arms and Max felt pretty good.

Until he looked at his phone.

Come over as soon as you get this. It's very important! Peregrine.

FOG AND MORE FOG ... IS THAT A BIG DOG?

Max stood on Peregrine's doorstep looking at the 'Have you seen this Puppy?' poster his friend was holding up for him to read, but trying to think of something less uncomfortable. It was funny, he thought to distract himself, that his friend practically lived at their house but he'd never been inside Peregrine's house – not once.

'Well?' Peregrine was looking a bit cross.

'Er, well, what?' asked Max back, playing for time.

'Have you seen this "puppy"?' Peregrine now looked cross and impatient.

'I, um…' Max made a show of peering at the quite-good pencil drawing of Sirius, as if he wasn't quite sure.

'Max!'

'OK, OK!' Max could tell pretty good fibs to strangers – like the one about Madame Pinky-Ponky getting her black belt in karate or that Frankenstein was half cheetah – but he was rubbish at telling lies to people he knew: they made him feel terrible. 'I was going to tell you, but I knew what you'd say.'

'I'd say...' said Peregrine, rubbing the top of his nose like head teachers do when they are trying to be patient with you (while showing how hard they are trying at the same time). 'I'd say, that you should have done what we agreed in the first place and returned him to his pack.'

'I tried,' Max protested, 'but he followed me home and then the weather got cold and I couldn't leave him outside all night – he's only a puppy – and anyway, I think they've gone...'

Peregrine held up a copy of the dreaded local paper, where all of Max's worst sins seemed to end up. It took him a few moments to scan the front page.

'Wolves,' said Peregrine, looking grim, 'in Oxfordshire.'

'OK, he goes back tomorrow,' Max agreed.

'It's probably too late for that.' Peregrine was rubbing his nose again. Uh, oh, thought Max. 'It looks like they've lost their fear of towns and, if you've got their cub, they'll know where to find us.'

'OK, so what should we do?' asked Max, beginning to get worried. He didn't mind telling his parents the truth but he did mind that they might be in danger.

'We get to your parents' house before they do,' said Peregrine, putting on his duffle jacket.

By now it was late. The firework displays were finished and most people had already walked home.

The streets were deathly quiet as a slow fog began to creep out of the park, roll across the main road and slip into side alleys. Max and Peregrine's footsteps echoed off brick walls that were covered in eerie shadows made by the flickering street lamps.

'It was a dark and scary night...' whispered Max and instead of telling him off, Peregrine just nodded and his fingers moved to the jacket pocket where he kept his best gadgets.

A quick clatter of footsteps behind them made Max spin around. He peered into the gloom, his heart beating fast … but it was just a couple crossing the road, their legs weirdly hidden by the fog so they looked cut in half.

Max shivered and it wasn't just the cold.

He jumped again as one of the dark shadows stretching across the wall moved. It crept away from the rest of the silhouettes and disappeared, as if something had slunk back into the fog as they approached. His monster ears picked up a faint scratching noise, like claws on concrete, claws that were trying not to make a sound.

Max swallowed and tried to keep calm.

He was just going to suggest to Peregrine about maybe walking quicker when they turned a corner and a dark blur ran into them.

'Ah!' cried Max.

'Oooofff!' said Peregrine, falling over. 'Watch out!'

'Get out of my way!' said the teenager who'd just collided with them. He scrabbled to his feet and Max could see he looked terrified. The boy ran off down the road.

The hair on the back of Max's neck stuck up as a low growl came from the darkened basement steps of a nearby house. Max's mouth went completely dry, his monster senses clanging in his head, telling him of extreme danger. The growl was answered by a long snarl from the other side of the street and the horrid sound of long claws clickity-clacking their scratchy way towards them.

'I think we're surrounded,' said Peregrine.

'I think I'm going to burp,' said Max.

'You do that, yes,' said Peregrine, as enthusiastically as you can when you are whispering out of the corner of your mouth.

A door banged open behind them, and they both twisted around in alarm.

But it was just two families leaving a café that was shutting up for the night. Max's Protect and Do Good Stuff distress signal said that, at all costs, whatever was growling and snarling could not be allowed to get past Max, down the road to those children and their unsuspecting parents.

Burp, he said to himself.

Nothing happened.

BURP!

Still nothing because it was incredibly difficult to burp when his mouth felt glued together.

'Max?'

Don't panic, Max thought. He scanned the fog, looking for clues. Nothing, it was deathly quiet and the fog, like the sea at low tide, was calm.

Max felt the hair on the back of his neck start to go back down. Whatever it was must have disappeared, slunk off, melted away, gone…

'RAAARRRR!'

The wolf leapt out of the fog where it had been hiding, all teeth, tail and red eyes in the night.

'WAAAA!' cried Max, taking in more air than he'd ever done in his life. Just in the nick of time, Max was ... MONSTER MAX!

'ROAR!' he roared and swiped at the wolf, who shot across the street and smashed into a wall.

'OW!' said Max – it had been like hitting an iron statue.

ZING! Peregrine had turned on his BUTT and become twenty feet tall with legs of steel just as another wolf jumped out of the fog, its teeth flashing white in the darkness. Peregrine kicked out and the wolf yelped. The wolf was strong enough to bend Peregrine's leg. (The metal one).

'Woooaw!' cried Peregrine, as he wobbled and fell over for the second time in less than two minutes.

More shapes started to appear: ridged black backs of fur sticking out of the mist, slicing through the fog like sharks through water, right towards where Peregrine lay in a tangled heap.

Max wasn't brilliant at maths but he did a quick calculation: with Peregrine down, there were too many enemies. Also, if they lost this fight, the werewolves would get to the house before Max could warn his parents.

RUN FOR IT.

'ROAR!' He roared one last roar, which did the trick. The wolves, unused to any sort of resistance, hesitated – they had seen their leader smashed against the wall by this big orange monster. Their delay bought Max precious seconds. He turned to Peregrine, grabbed the one remaining metal leg, and snapped it off.

'Grery sorry!' he said. Then he slung Peregrine over his shoulder and bounded off into the night. Faster, he hoped, than any wolf could follow.

As the wolves' howls of rage and frustration that they'd lost their prey faded into the fog, Monster Max slowed and turned for home.

Just before he got to their street, he put Peregrine down.

'Grot, any sneezing powder? Grine's run out.'

Peregrine fished about in another one of his large pockets.

'Here you go … and thanks for saving me,' he added. 'Those wolves are something else.'

'Atchoo! Yup, you can say that again,' said Max.

'Those wolves are something else.'

'Oh, ha ha,' said Max, 'very funny. Tell you what, let me tell the jokes and you can stick to figuring out what to do about … Mum!'

'What?' asked Peregrine, who was standing behind Max as they walked towards Max's parents' front door. 'Max? What do we need to do about your mum, she's fine? Actually … oh, I see.'

Peregrine took a couple of paces back behind Max, who was staring at his mother.

Who was standing on the doorstep.

Looking furious.

Holding Sirius in her arms.

7

ONCE AGAIN, MAX HAS A LOT OF EXPLAINING TO DO

Max looked back, but Peregrine had disappeared. (He didn't blame him.) He turned back to his mother and looked at Sirius who wagged his curly tail and yapped excitedly.

'I'm a lot more angry than disappointed,' said his mother, who was definitely quite scary when she was cross. Her eyes flashed silver-grey and Sirius, suddenly sensing the wolf in her, whined. 'Kitchen, now,' she said and turned.

Five minutes later, Max looked at the stern faces of his parents across the table and tried to ignore Sirius, who was very busy chewing and licking his fingers. He knew he had a lot of explaining to do and he'd have to say sorry: that was bad but not half as bad as it could have been if he'd got to his parents too late and the Varkas pack was already there.

'You've got a lot of explaining to do.' His mother stirred her tea crossly and his dad nodded.

So Max took a deep breath. He told them about the first night at the dump, the short fight with the Varkas pack, taking the cub back to the dump but that not working out as planned, the longer fight earlier that evening in the fog with the Varkas pack again. He also mentioned (as if he really needed to) that Sirius was really cute and that, in his opinion, werewolves made excellent pets and everyone should have one. Then he saw the look on his parents' faces and added that he was sorry – really, really sorry – for all the trouble he had caused.

And he made sure he got in that neither Peregrine nor Frankenstein had anything to do with any of it.

After a short pause, his parents looked at each other, then back to Max.

'OK, we can understand how it happened,' his dad said. 'It's not telling the truth that is the worst thing in all this. You're not little anymore, Max, so you do know that, don't you?'

'Yes,' said Max unhappily. 'I'm sorry I told fibs, but sometimes they're useful. Everybody does it...'

'...and that's wrong,' his mother interrupted sharply. 'Fibs might seem like a good idea at the time, but they always make things worse in the end.'

'I know,' said Max. 'I really am sorry.'

Both parents began to look a little less cross with him.

'Well, I'm going out tonight and I'm handing him back myself,' said his mother firmly. 'The Varkas pack hasn't attacked yet, but they will. Having their cub back may mean they're less angry... And he does seem very fond of you, so it's obvious you've been taking good care of him, which is something.'

'Wait, what, no!' Max was just about to say that there was no way he was going to let his mum go out alone and meet the wolves, it was far too dangerous (and if anyone was going to hand Sirius back and say goodbye properly, it was going to be him) when Madame Pinky-Ponky came in, which was just as well as he was pretty sure saying all that to his mum in the mood she was in would cause a proper argument.

Madame Pinky-Ponky looked worried.

'There are people surrounding the house in the fog,' she said. 'Except I know they're not ordinary people.'

Just then the bell went and Max

realised two things: one, he really didn't want his mother to answer the door on her own and, two, Sirius had stopped licking his fingers.

Max got to the door just as his mother opened it to reveal a very large man with a pointy beard standing on their doorstep. It was freezing outside, but the man wore only a tattered T-shirt. Underneath the ripped cloth, his knotted muscles moved about like fat snakes in a bag. His huge arms and the backs of his hands were covered in hair and his eyes flashed red as he stared at Max's mum.

Max cleared his throat. 'Mum…'

She ignored him. His mum stood very still, staring up at the man, letting the silence between her and the stranger build until the tension hummed in the air. 'So we both know who each of us is now,' she said eventually.

'Yes,' said the man, obviously not someone who was comfortable talking. 'We follow his scent,' he pointed at Max, 'to here, then smell yours.'

'Mum…'

'Don't do anything hasty, like turning into a monster, Max,' whispered his dad, who was just behind him. Max shook his head.

'There's just something I need to… Mum?'

'There's nothing for you here, except what is already yours.' His mother was still ignoring Max. 'Whatever Fanghorn has sent you for is none of your business. It's between him and me.'

'Give me the cub,' the half-man, half-wolf growled. Behind him, in the fog,

Max could see other shapes: some wolf, some human. It felt like they were all waiting for the signal to attack.

'He is yours,' said Max's mum, 'but I need your promise you'll leave if I do.'

'Give me the cub,' said the man, his sharp teeth pale in the moonlight. The shapes moved closer.

'Mum!' Max really couldn't wait any longer.

'What!' The Varkas pack leader, and his mum and his dad all stared crossly at Max for interrupting their grown-up wolf-on-wolf standoff.

Max looked at the man and the pack gathering behind him and wondered if he shouldn't just burp. Instead he said to him, 'We don't have Sirius.'

'Who?'

'I mean your cub.'

The change in the giant person on their doorstep was instant. Max had no time to burp as one moment there was a very strong and hairy man who wasn't very chatty on their doorstep, the next there was a huge black wolf.

But his mum moved like lightning, too, slamming the door and turning to Max.

'What do you mean, we don't have Sirius?'

'I was trying to tell you. One minute he was there,' said Max, 'the next he'd disappeared.'

'Give me my son!' the wolf roared on the other side of the door, 'or I will smash your house down!'

'We don't have him!' said Max's mum.

'You lie!'

'No, it's true,' cried Max. 'We had him but we don't anymore!'

'I don't believe you. Fanghorn said not to trust you! I will give you to the count of ten to bring him to me or you will be sorry! One!'

'Quick,' said the mum. 'Both of you upstairs. I'll hold them off.'

'Oh no, you won't!' said Max's dad.

'Ditto,' said Max, getting ready to burp.

'Snap,' said Madame Pinky-Ponky, who'd finally made it into the hall.

'Two!'

Max's mum's hand moved slowly towards the door latch. Max knew then and there she was going to open the door, leap out and try and fight the Varkas pack leader on her own.

'Three!'

Max got ready to burp. He would jump over her and block the door, then she'd have to save his dad and Madame Pinky-Ponky.

'Four!'

He knew it was a terrible plan, but everything was happening rather quickly and he didn't have time to think up another one.

'Five!'

Max took a deep breath. Ready ... steady ... bur...

Just then he heard a step on the stairs and someone cleared their throat. In an annoying way.

'You lot. I leave you alone for ten minutes and you've got a pack of howling wolves huffing and puffing, threatening to blow the door down.'

Peregrine stood at the top of the landing with Frankenstein, looking rather pleased with himself.

'What are you waiting for?' he grinned, as Max, Max's mum and dad and Madame Pinky-Ponky just stood there, gawping at him. 'The tunnel in the cellar will get us almost all the way to my new Secret Lair. You can thank Frankenstein for discovering it.'

'Six!'

'Well, what are we waiting for?' said Max's dad.

SECRET LAIRS AND ANGRY WERES

'But we can't leave before we know where Sirius is!' Max protested, as they hurried through the library.

From downstairs and outside they heard. 'Ten!' The Varkas pack leader's voice now sounded less human, more howl. 'I shall blow wwwwooooooo this house down. Wooooooooooooooooooooo!' and all around came answering calls from the others in the pack.

'There's no time, Max!' His father looked really sorry. 'Sirius almost certainly joined his pack when they turned up at the house. They are his family after all.'

'Miaow,' said Frankenstein, looking like he was trying to tell them something.

As they hesitated by the secret door in the library that led to the cellar, they heard their front door splintering.

'I just painted that,' his dad said unhappily.

'I think we should go right now,' said Peregrine.

'Miaow,' said Frankenstein again. But no one was listening.

There were several tunnels in the cellar connecting one part of the house to another. Max's house was far bigger on the inside than anyone on the outside suspected. However, one tunnel – the one Max and Peregrine had used to capture the Grimp on their first-ever mission – led away from the house, towards the centre of old Oxford.

It was this twisting tunnel they took.

After a short while, they came across a new pile of rubble and a fork in the passageway heading away from town.

'This is new.' Max's mum stared about as she helped Madame Pinky-Ponky along and Max could tell she could see in the dark with her wolf's eyes.

'I saw Frankenstein coming out of a small hole earlier and it was easy to make the hole bigger so that I could explore. It's the perfect escape tunnel, as it goes out of town, to the Lair – but it must have been here for centuries,' Peregrine said, taking out something that looked like one of those penknives that have lots of useful tools. Except this one contained a torch. Peregrine switched it on.

It sent out a narrow beam that just

about lit their way, but left lots of space in the tunnel for dark patches and wobbly shadows. The walls were made of stone and had swirly carvings and intricate patterns.

'We really must get around to exploring the tunnels one day, Max,' said his dad.

'Er,' said Max, who didn't like dark places, cobwebs or not being able to see around corners. 'No.'

He saw Peregrine, who was walking beside him, roll his eyes.

'Sorry,' said Max.

Peregrine looked a bit surprised. 'What for?'

'This is probably all my fault for keeping quiet about Sirius – you know, wolves chasing us, Dad's smashed front door, your broken BUTT.'

'I think they'd be after us anyway,' said Peregrine. 'This Fanghorn really doesn't seem to like your family much. Stealing Sirius probably made them a lot crosser. I reckon they're going to eat us. Except Frankenstein – I don't think he's digestible.'

'Thanks,' said Max. 'You're a real comfort, you know that?'

'I just get up every morning and try my best to make the world a better place,' said Peregrine modestly.

'Got any plans?'

'Well.' Peregrine took a deep breath. 'I think we should make it up as we go along. You're pretty good at that and it's always worked out so far.'

'OK,' said Max, unsure and still feeling guilty. Peregrine was trying to make him feel better, which was nice, but wasn't really working.

DONK!

Max banged his head, which brought him out of his gloomy thoughts. They had come to the end of the tunnel.

Peregrine shone the small torch along the side of the wall, the beam stopping at an old metal ladder.

'Here we are,' he said, and started to climb.

A few moments later and they had all followed Peregrine up the ladder (everyone trying to help Madame Pinky-Ponky, who shoo'd them away because she was 'just fine') and through the twisted stems of a bush that disguised the exit of the tunnel.

It was still foggy here, but Max felt glad to be outside again. He looked around.

'I can't see the Secret Lair Treehouse,' he remarked.

'That's the whole point,' Peregrine said, fiddling about with what appeared to be a small tree. 'Otherwise it would be called "The Obvious Lair Treehouse".'

'OK, I give up. Where's the ladder, then?'

'There is no ladder.'

'Really?' Max's dad was intrigued. They all watched with interest as Peregrine bent the tree back with a series of ropes and pulleys, until its top touched the ground. A small sack, big enough to sit in, dropped down. There was a satisfying click and Peregrine let go of the bent tree with its basket.

'Ta da!' he said. 'It's the Secret Peregrine Long-arc Trebuchet. Instead of a ladder, which is hard to disguise (and boring), you get up to the Lair Treehouse by catapult.'

'SPLAT,' muttered Max, and Madame Pinky-Ponky prodded it suspiciously with her walking stick.

'Me first!' said Max's mum.

The SPLAT (Secret Peregrine Long-arc Trebuchet) machine worked brilliantly.

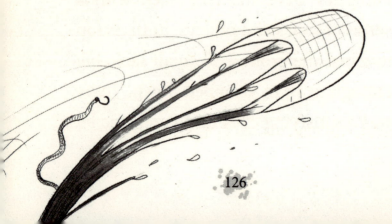

Even Max had to admit it when it was his turn. Peregrine released the lever and Max sailed high into the frosty night air with Frankenstein clinging to his head. They both landed, very comfortably, in a large net strung high up between several trees.

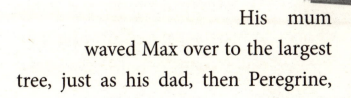

His mum waved Max over to the largest tree, just as his dad, then Peregrine, came flying over the treetops and landed bouncily nearby. Being catapulted helped to put them all back in a better mood – because having to escape a pack of very angry werewolves is going to ruin most people's evening.

They all clambered over to find this particular tree had a comfortable room with some hammocks and a cosy-looking fireplace.

'Wow,' said Max's mum. 'Peregrine, you really are a genius. This is lovely.'

'Thank you. It's very basic, really,' said Peregrine, graciously. 'I think we can risk a fire, to get us all warmed up. I'll sort that out…'

'And I've bought tea bags and some chocolate biscuits,' piped up Madame Pinky-Ponky, who would somehow manage to bring something delicious along even if she got abducted by aliens and dropped into a black hole.

Ten minutes later, the treehouse was warming up nicely. They drank their tea while Peregrine showed them his control console that dropped down from the ceiling on wooden cogs.

'There are six trees in the Lair, each with its own look-out point and lighting. No nails or saws were used to damage the trees, it's just roped together and water is gathered from rain in the canopy above. We've got thermal imaging, radar and this is the defence system … Max!'

'Ouch!'

'No touching. I've booby-trapped the

woods below, and can arm them by pressing this big red button. Otherwise, it's perfectly safe to stroll about around here. And this,' Peregrine pointed at a silver lever, 'was what I was working on recently. It shuts up the entire cabin in metal casing – like a sort of aerial panic room.'

'What are the other trees for?' Max's dad looked like Christmas had come early.

'Mainly research, but I can cover the netting in the middle and have a workshop area when I need to build something really big … in secret.'

This was great, thought Max, as he finished his tea and the others all carried on asking Peregrine questions and thanking him. But he began to think about why they were here in the first place. Whatever Peregrine said, it still felt like it was all his fault they had to go into hiding, leaving wolves running around their house, but everyone was too nice to say so.

And that made him feel terrible.

Then he thought about Sirius and felt even worse. His tea suddenly tasted cold and bitter.

Perhaps the small cub wasn't with his family. Perhaps he was somewhere out in the cold and the fog, all on his own.

Max remembered Frankenstein miaowing a lot before they left the house in such a hurry. What was that all about? He looked around, expecting to see Frankenstein by the fire, but he wasn't there. Nor was he curled up in one of the hammocks.

'Er…' Max didn't like to interrupt Peregrine's moment of glory but… 'Has anyone seen Frankenstein?'

'Not since we first got up here,' admitted his mum.

'Anyone else?' asked Max.

'Non.'

'Nope.'

'Sorry, no, me neither,' said his dad, as everyone started to look around.

I'm rubbish at pets, thought Max. They keep running off. They must hate me.

'I've got to go and look around the woods,' he said, forgetting he was scared of the dark. 'Mum, can you help me? And Peregrine, can you use your radar? Peregrine?'

But his friend was already using the radar: in fact, he was staring hard at the screen, a worried look on his face. And Max didn't need to ask why. His monster hearing had just picked up the sound of running paws, panting and snarls.

'They've found us,' he said. 'But how?'

'I'm not surprised,' said his mother. 'A few of the pack leaders must have followed our scent into the tunnel. They'll know where we are, and so we need to protect ourselves right now. Max...'

'Already on it,' said Max, burping.

'Stay by me all the time,' his mother said, turning into a wolf. 'These wolves are strong. Wait, Max!'

But Max had already made up his mind what he was going to do. Before anyone could stop him, he sped across the room with all his monster speed, pulled the metal lever so hard he snapped it off and jumped through the window just before the metal shutters came crashing down.

Those metal shutters are probably just as good at keeping people in as out, he thought, as he crashed through the branches towards the forest floor. This was his problem and he would sort it out himself.

Monster Max landed with his best Hero Landing, stood tall and roared his roariest roar … as the first wolves charged.

BATTLE

The pack leader leaped high and Max ducked at the very last second, as another two wolves sprang out of what remained of the fog.

Max roared again and batted them away with the back of his hand, but he was careful to keep his claws in.

Because Max had just made another very important decision: he wasn't going to hurt any of the Varkas pack. They were only trying to get their cub back. He was hoping he could fight them until they got tired and decided to talk.

Six more wolves split from the pack. Large, black and very fast, they slid through the trees until they were right behind Max. And they would have been on him if Peregrine and his Secret Lair defence system hadn't sprung into action. There was a sudden flash and they were blinded by two very bright lights, which gave Max time to leap over them, grab them from behind and tie their tails together in super-fast monster style.

He turned, but just too late, as four more of the pack jumped on top of him. Max wobbled, smelling disgusting doggy breath in his face, seeing flashes of teeth.

SQUEAK   SQUEAK   SQUEAKY SQUEAK!

Loudspeakers hidden in the trees were making squeaky toy sounds.

All four wolves suddenly stopped and looked up.

Max remembered his dad saying wolves loved rubber toys. Pushing the distracted wolves away, he took a huge breath and jumped high, scattering the wolves, who were still trying to see where the squeaky toy was.

Unfortunately he landed right in the middle of the rest of the pack.

Twelve sets of very large teeth snarled at him as the wolves crept towards Monster Max and Max snarled back, showing an even bigger set of teeth ... then decided to jump up a tree. Unfortunately, he'd changed into a monster a bit too quickly and part of what remained of his (second favourite) pair of underpants were still attached to him.

As he bounded up, the biggest wolf reached out and grabbed at Max. His long wolf teeth snagging on the pants…

Now, people who discuss the 'Battle of Monster Max v the Varkas Pack' afterwards will not be able to agree on who enjoyed the underpants experience less: Monster Max, who tried jumping up and down through the forest with a wolf attached to his shaggy bottom; or the wolf who found himself stuck to Max's behind and bounced through rough trees, thorny bushes, patches of nettles and small, pointy rocks all with a pair of grubby pants in his mouth. The poor wolf tried letting go, but the pants had surprisingly strong elastic which had wrapped around his long teeth.

Eventually the elastic did snap and the wolf bounced away into the night.

But he still has nightmares about it.

And so the battle went on: wolves charged Monster Max and Max did his best to avoid them and avoid hurting them. Peregrine's defence systems were a big help – especially the custard bombs, although Max was probably a lot more scared of the clockwork spiders Peregrine released than the six-foot werewolves.

Eventually, bit by slow bit, Peregrine's

defences ran out and Monster Max got more and more (and more) tired.

His arms felt like lumps of stone and his legs hadn't the energy to jump higher than a few feet. The Varkas pack, sensing weakness, began to close in.

'Roar!' roared Max, but even that wasn't very impressive anymore. He wondered what his parents, Madame Pinky-Ponky and Peregrine must be thinking, stuck up there unable to do anything. The wolves were really close now, all twenty of them and all getting ready to spring.

Oh dear, thought Max. I've really messed it up this time and he barely had time to finish the thought before he was covered with wolves and he began to sink to his knees under the weight of them.

His mum must be worried.

It all seemed a bit hopeless and Max really had no idea what to do…

Hisss, spit! Hisss.

A familiar sound penetrated the mass of bodies and a chink of moonlight appeared in front of Max's eyes. Several wolves yelped, followed by much more hissing and spitting. It took Monster Max a moment to figure out what was going on. Then he realised…

Frankenstein!

The pack scattered as Max saw Frankenstein leap from one wolf to the other, scratching and biting. They'd fought Rock Giants and Ice Witches but none of them had come up against anything quite as sneaky and ferocious as Max's cat.

As one, the pack turned on this new threat. Frankenstein might be tough but one good mouthful would be all they needed.

Monster Max suddenly saw the terrible danger Frankenstein was in. No! he thought. No, no, no, nononono. NO!

He took a deep breath and burped once, twice, and then again, growing each time.

He turned, claws like scimitars glinting in the moon.

'DON'T YOU HURT MY CAT!' bellowed Monster Max.

Sixteen remaining wolves, including the leader, swung back round to this new ferocious Monster Max, fear showing in their eyes for the very first time. But they were proud warriors, the fiercest fighters from Krit, and they would not run.

Thirty-two back legs like steel springs prepared to jump...

'Yap, yap, (mini) snarl, yap, (mini) grrrrrrrr, yap...'

Between Max and the wolves, a small shape appeared. A small, fluffy shape, with sticky-up ears and a waggy tail.

10

GOODBYE ... FOR NOW

All the werewolves hesitated, especially the two at the front.

It was clear that Sirius was blocking their path to Monster Max, as if to say: 'If you want to get to him, you'll have to go through me.'

Sirius was protecting him.

Slowly, as if swathed in smoke, a sleek wolf crouching next to the Varkas pack leader changed into the human form of a tall woman with long, black hair.

Sirius ran to his mother and she picked him up with tears in her eyes.

She stared at her cub for a long time and it seemed to Max they were somehow talking to one another – with expressions and small sounds he couldn't quite hear.

All the while, the other wolves watched and waited.

Eventually, she turned to Max who stood there, shaggy, panting and very tired … and she smiled. She cleared her throat, as if she wasn't used to talking.

'Over the past few weeks, we've come to love it here in England. There's no Fanghorn for starters. You see, we don't just follow orders, whatever Fanghorn would like to think, so we decided to stay, but then we lost our cub.'

'I'm grerry shorry,' said Monster Max. 'I didn't mean to take him…'

'I know,' the tall woman said. 'We know. My son says you didn't steal him but that you looked after him. He also says you saved his life … twice … although I'm not sure if I believe the stuff about flying rockets…'

'Err,' said Monster Max, 'he's probably gre-xaggerating a bit – cubs, eh?'

There was a crunching metal sound and something lithe, powerful and grey landed softly next to Monster Max.

'Oh grello, Mum,' said Max.

All the wolves tensed but no one moved. Instead they looked at each other for a long while in silence: a lone grey wolf facing a pack of Varkas wolves with burning red eyes.

Eventually, his mother seemed to lift her head and straighten, as the pack leader, still in wolf form, did the same. And just like that there were two more humans standing in the colourless dawn light.

'Greverythings alright now, Mum,' said Max.

'Yes,' she said turning to him. 'You're not hurt, are you? That was a very stupid but very brave thing to do, Max.' She had tears in her eyes. 'I'm very proud of you.' She turned to the Varkas pack, who were all now changing to human form. 'Would anyone like a nice cup of tea?'

Some time later, they were sitting at the edge of the woods outside Oxford, watching a pale winter sun rise above the frosty countryside: Max, his parents, Madame Pinky-Ponky, Peregrine and the whole of the Varkas pack.

This was not how Max thought the night would end, but he was glad it had turned out like this.

And there wasn't just tea because Peregrine had stocked the Lair with about a year's supply of baked beans and frankfurters in tins that they heated over a fire as they talked about the battle.

'When you did a triple somersault and tied our tails together, that was the best bit,' said a very square man with long moustaches, grinning at Max, who was back to normal too.

'I think the way you hide in fog and pounce out snarling just when everyone least expects is brilliant,' Max told him.

'Aw, thanks,' said the man, unable to stop himself grinning proudly. 'Really? I mean it's not too corny, a bit obvious or anything? That's what we were worried about, weren't we, lads?'

'Yeah!'

'No, not at all,' said Peregrine, coming over. 'It was totally surprising and super-scary.'

'Yup!' said Max. 'New pants all round.'

'Shucks!' their new friend said. 'You guys are the best enemies.'

After they had finished, everyone helped tidy up the paper plates and wooden cutlery, which they burned on the fire so there was no mess.

The Varkas pack leaders, Razortooth and his wife Moonsong, came over.

'We must go now,' said Moonsong, 'but thank you again. And thank you to your brave cat, Frankenstein. Our son told us everything about how, when we came to your house, he'd thought he was in trouble with us for running off, so he hid in one of your tunnels. Then you left without him, so Frankenstein came back – even though he doesn't like him – found out where he was hiding and brought him to us.'

Max glanced at where Frankenstein was hanging out with the wolves, looking like he was having a great time and smiled. When Frankenstein had turned up with Sirius (just in time) Max guessed something like that must have happened. Good old Frankenstein – he really had been trying to tell them something before they left the house in such a hurry after all.

'So are you definitely not going back to Krit?' Max turned back to Sirius' parents.

'No,' said Razortooth, somewhat savagely, 'not whilst Fanghorn is in charge. We've made up our minds.'

'So where are you going to go?' asked Max's dad.

'We'll go where there are fewer people. We prefer it that way,' said Razortooth.

Just then, Sirius came bounding over, his tail wagging madly, and Moonsong picked him up. She smiled again and looked at Max.

'I hear you called him Sirius – after the star?' she said.

'Oh, yes, sorry about that,' replied Max. 'I didn't know his name and I don't understand wolf, so I had to make something up.'

'Well, we think it's an excellent name,' she said, smiling. 'So it's what we will call our son from now. In honour of you, Monster Max!'

Max looked around and saw the pack was starting to move off.

'I guess this is goodbye?' He reached out and stroked one of Sirius' soft ears, feeling suddenly very sad.

'Yes,' said Moonsong, 'but I think we'll be seeing you again. When you need us, we will come.'

And with that, the Varkas pack melted into the dawn, as silently as only wolves, even in human form, can.

'Well,' said Max's dad as they walked down the hill back home, 'we were cross about Sirius, and I'm sure you've learned not to tell fibs but it turns out you were right to help him, Max. I guess the point is always to follow your instincts, even if some people think you're wrong. If you're sure you are doing right (and you'll probably know), then tell people why. If they care about you, then they'll listen and it'll all work out – it usually does. Well done … well done to you too, Peregrine.'

'Thanks, Dad,' said Max. 'Sorry, I lied.'

'Yes, thanks, Mr Forbes. I'll help you repair your front door if you don't mind explaining to my parents why I need a sheet of re-enforced steel without actually telling them it's to repair the Treehouse Lair I've built in the woods.'

'Deal,' said his dad.

They walked along in silence for a bit, exhausted but happy.

Without his elite wolves to fight for him, they wouldn't be hearing from Fanghorn for a long time.

EPILOGUE

Far, far away, dawn was rising over the misty peak of Krit.

Fanghorn stared out across the dark forest that surrounded his castle.

He should have heard from the Varkas pack by now. They should have brought him the boy Max and his mother.

But, like the shadows under the trees that melted away in the coming morning light, they had gone.

Fanghorn raised his head and howled in anger.

Monster Max and the Bobble Hat of Forgetting
BOOK ONE

7-9 | PB | £6.99 | ISBN 9781913102333

Max is an unusual 9-year-old. He can turn himself
into a huge, bin-eating monster by BURPING.
Being a monster is brilliant, unless he sneezes
(which turns him back) and he finds himself far
from home in just his pants.

Max decides to be more responsible and 'protect
and do good stuff', starting with catching a local
vandal. But his nemesis, Peregrine, is convinced
Max is the vandal, and invents his POOP (Portable
Operating Omni Prison) machine to trap him. If
Peregrine can prove the truth, Max and his mother
could be put in a zoo … or worse. Max will have to
use his wits as well as his strength to catch the real
culprit, before Peregrine can catch him…

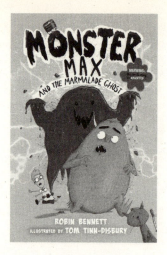

Monster Max and the Marmalade Ghost
BOOK TWO

7-9 | PB | £6.99 | ISBN 9781913102821

Max is an ordinary boy, except that he can turn into a monster when he burps…

Max and Peregrine are volunteering at an old people's home, when strange things start to happen. One resident is walking on the ceiling, one is riding their wheelchair through walls, and Reggie says his marmalade is haunted (no one listens). Can Max and his friends work out what's happening to protect his family and the local community? Things aren't looking good: the Marmalade Ghost is turning into a sticky Godzilla, Max falls out with his (joint) best friend, and then just when it can't get any worse, someone kidnaps Max's cat, Frankenstein…

Time to 'Protect and Do Good Stuff!